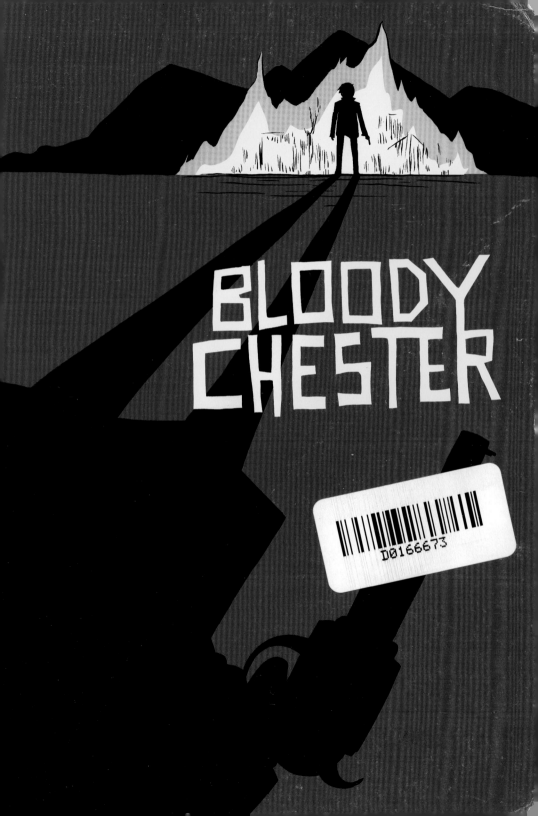

BLOODY CHESTER

written by **JT Petty**

illustrated by **Hilary Florido**

colored by **Hilary Sycamore**

:01

First Second

new york & london

For Sarah, who carries the ax.
—JT Petty

Thank you to my family, friends, and
Bob for all your help and support.
—Hilary Florido

8

19

21

25

HEY. YOU
ALIVE?

37

GO UP THE TRAIL WEST OF TOWN. THERE'S A FLAT ROCK WITH AN EMPTY BASKET ON IT AT THE TOP. LEAVE THAT ONE AND BRING BACK T'OTHER.

THERE'S A SIGN HANGING ON A . . . ON THE EDGE OF TOWN THAT SAYS "COYOTE WAITS."

THAT'S THE PLAGUE. IT'S AN INDIAN DISEASE.

MY MOMMA WAS ONE OF THE FIRST TO DIE OF IT. ME AND THAT BOY, POTTER, ARE THE ONLY ONES SEEM TO BE IMMUNE.

WHAT ABOUT THE PREACHER?

HE'S DYING OF IT.

HOW DO YOU GET IT?

NOBODY KNOWS. IT DOESN'T SHOW ITSELF UNTIL IT'S TOO LATE. HIDES IN YOUR BELLY FOR A LONG TIME. S'WHY THEY CALL IT "WAITS."

EVERYBODY WHO'S GOT IT WAS FINE ONE DAY AND DEAD THE NEXT.

GO ON AND EAT. YOU ALREADY GOT ANYTHING IT'S GONNA GIVE.

SIP.

. . .

WHERE'S THE BOY?

43

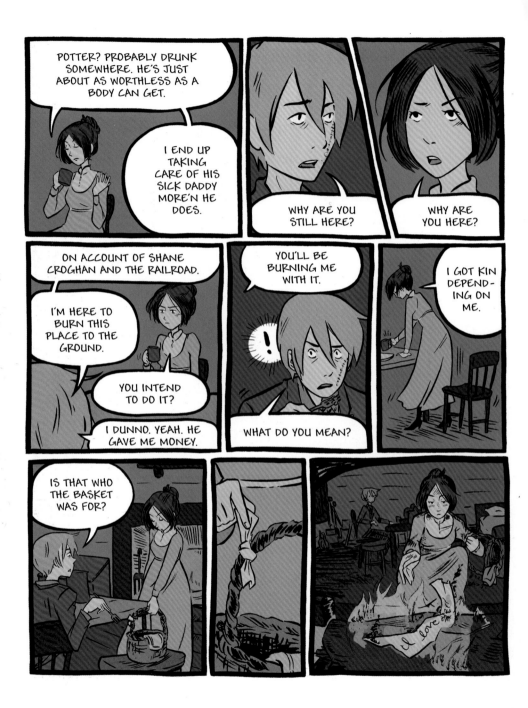

45

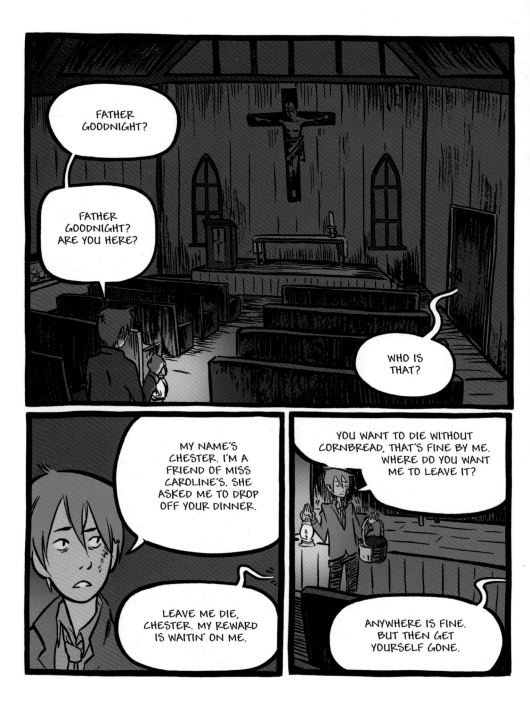

FATHER GOODNIGHT?

FATHER GOODNIGHT? ARE YOU HERE?

WHO IS THAT?

MY NAME'S CHESTER. I'M A FRIEND OF MISS CAROLINE'S. SHE ASKED ME TO DROP OFF YOUR DINNER.

LEAVE ME DIE, CHESTER. MY REWARD IS WAITIN' ON ME.

YOU WANT TO DIE WITHOUT CORNBREAD, THAT'S FINE BY ME. WHERE DO YOU WANT ME TO LEAVE IT?

ANYWHERE IS FINE. BUT THEN GET YOURSELF GONE.

47

48

57

62

WHAT'S SHE DOING WITH THAT AX?

HER DADDY'S CRAZY.

PROBABLY RUNS IN THE FAMILY. THAT AND CUSSEDNESS.

MISS CAROLINE BARBER? SHE'S CRAZY.

SHE'S SMASHED HOLES IN JUST ABOUT EVERY BUILDING IN TOWN.

THINK SHE'S LOOKING FOR SOMETHING?

TREASURE, I EXPECT. THAT OR MAYBE HER DADDY'S MARBLES.

HOW D'YOU GET IT?

I DON'T GOT IT!

I MEANT HOW DOES A BODY GET IT?

IT'S A DISEASE OF THE SPIRIT.

GHOSTS.

YOU MEAN DEAD MEN?

I MEAN THEIR SPIRITS. WHATEVER'S THE SAME BETWEEN A DEAD MAN AND A LIVING IS WHAT GETS INFECTED.

AND AS LONG AS THOSE SPIRITS ARE AROUND, IT'LL KEEP SPREADING.

WE JUST GOTTA PUT ALL THESE MEN IN THE GROUND, GIVE THEM A CHRISTIAN BURIAL.

IT'S THEIR BODIES THAT ROTTED, NOT THEIR GHOSTS.

IT WAS THEIR GHOSTS. IT BURNT 'EM UP FROM THE INSIDE IN LEAVING.

SUIT YERSELF. WE GOTTA MAKE MR. HARKEY A CROSS.

YOU KNEW HIM?

SURE. I LIVE HERE. I KNEW ALL THESE FOLKS, SAVE THE INDIANS.

AND I S'POSE THE CHINAMEN WEREN'T NONE FRIENDLY, BUT I'D SEEN 'EM AROUND.

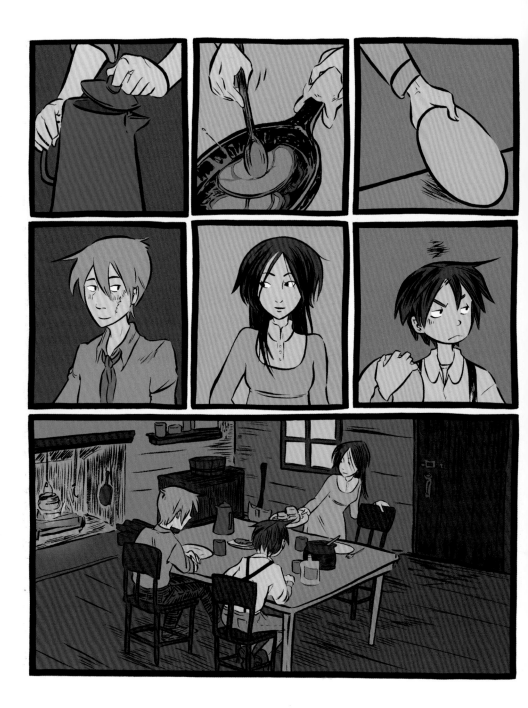

I WAS JUST IN ROUGH SHAPE WHEN I SHOWED UP IN THE TOWN OF AVERILL A COUPLE MONTHS BACK, SO SOMEBODY GAVE ME THAT NAME.

AND I WAS NEVER A BAD MAN,

I JUST GOT A REPUTATION FOR IT ON ACCOUNT OF MY NAME.

AVERILL'S A FAIR ROWDY PLACE, SO A TOUGH REPUTATION WASN'T A BAD THING TO HAVE.

TAP

BUT IT WASN'T A REPUTATION I WAS PARTICULAR PROUD OF.

IT LASTED FOR A FEW MONTHS, UNTIL I STARTED TO COURT THIS SCHOOLTEACHER I MET AT CHURCH.

SHE SEEMED LIKE A NICE GIRL, UNTIL I . . .

. . . MET HER PARENTS.

Click.

I NEVER HAVE.

I TOLD HER MY FAMILY NAME. WHICH IS KATES.

SHE WAS THE FIRST GIRL WHOSE PARENTS I'D MET, AND I GUESS SHE MADE ME NERVOUS.

I'M CHESTER KATES.

I GUESS THE NEXT DAY SHE TOLD EVERYBODY, CAUSE THEY STOPPED CALLING ME BLOODY CHESTER.

I'D GOTTEN USED TO BEING A BAD MAN BY THAT POINT,

AND MY PRIDE WOULDN'T ALLOW ME TO IGNORE BEING CALLED . . . THAT.

AVERILL'S A PRETTY TOUGH TOWN.

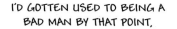

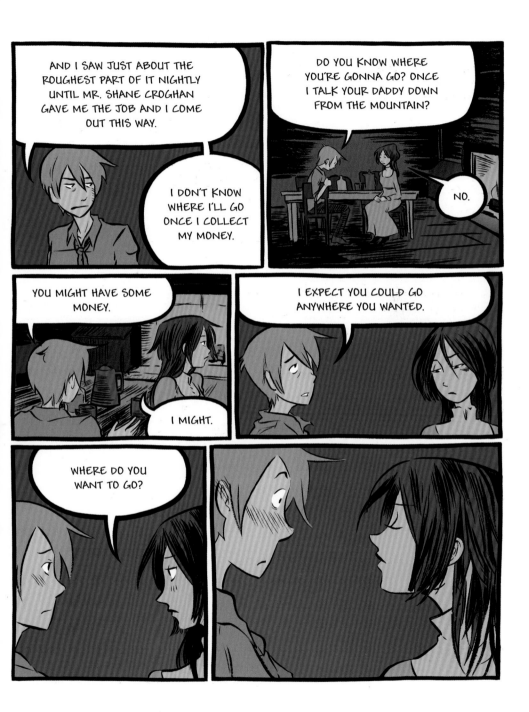

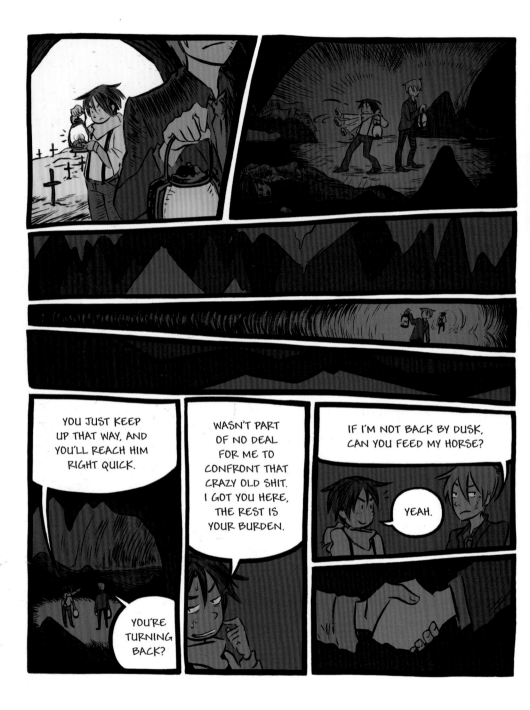

94

102

NO, SIR.

WELL YOU LIKELY ALREADY DONE IT. BROUGHT MY OWN HOUNDS AROUND TO FEED ON ME.

WHO WERE YE SHOOTIN' AT?

I WOULDA THOUGHT THEY WERE FRIENDS OF YOURS. OR YOUR GHOSTS.

OR WHATEVER THEY ARE, I CAIN'T BARELY SEE ANY MORE. SHOWED UP EVER' NIGHT SINCE YOU DID.

PROBABLY AFTER MY CLAIM, SAME AS YOU. BUT YOU'LL HAVE TO BURY ME IN THIS GROUND 'FORE YOU TAKE ANYTHING OUT OF IT.

I DON'T WANT YOUR CLAIM, NOR ANY OF THE GOLD YOU HID DOWN IN WHALE.

DRINK SOME WATER.

DON'T TOUCH ME! DON'T YOU FUCKIN' BREATHE ON ME, YOU DRIZZLIN' SHIT!

YOU'VE TAKEN TO THE COYOTE! I CAN SEE THE SICKNESS ON YOU.

IF I HAD IT, I'D BE DEAD.

IT AIN'T THAT SIMPLE. COYOTE WAITS. IT'S IN WHAT THEY CALL SIDIOUS.

YOU SEEN THE BODIES?

I SEEN SOME.

MY WIFE WAS ONE OF THE FIRST TO TAKE SICK AND DIE. WE FOUND HER ROTTED OUT LIKE A BURNT HOUSE.

DAVIS, THE COOPER'S BOY, DIED THE DAY FOLLOWING,

DIDN'T LOOK LIKE THE CYANIDE BURNS AT ALL.

AND MELODY GRIEVE THE DAY AFTER THAT.

I NEVER TOUCHED A ONE OF THEM. NOR THE DOZENS OF THE NEXT MONTH.

WHAT ABOUT CAROLINE?

DOES SHE KNOW IT AIN'T REAL?

IT'S REAL.

DOES SHE KNOW IT'S YOUR DOIN'?

YOU DON'T TELL HER THAT. YOU DON'T BREATHE A FUCKIN' WORD.

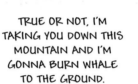

TRUE OR NOT, I'M TAKING YOU DOWN THIS MOUNTAIN AND I'M GONNA BURN WHALE TO THE GROUND.

AND THAT'S A GODDAMNED FACT.

HOW'S FIRE GONNA STOP A PLAGUE COUCHED IN MEN'S IMAGINATION?

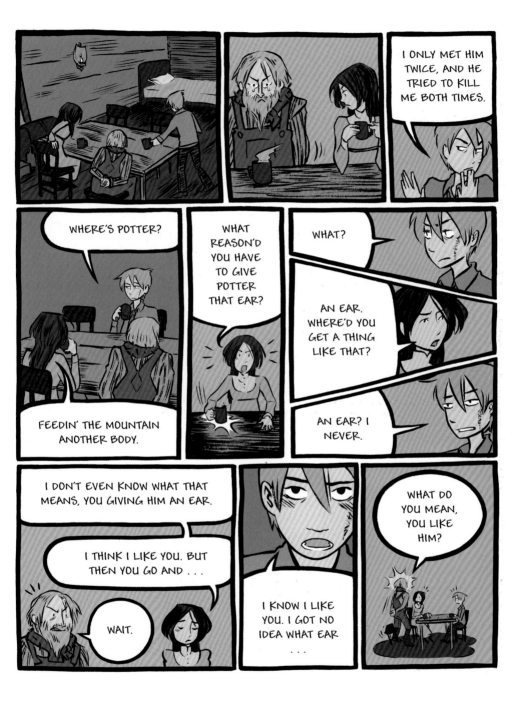

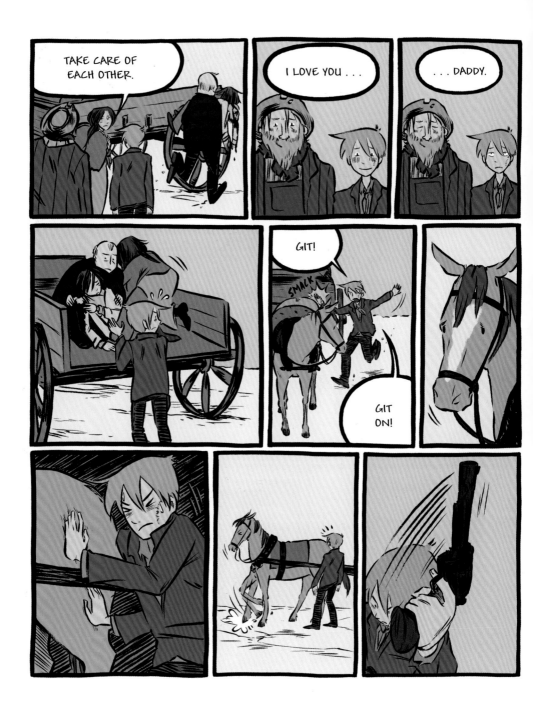

THE HOTEL!

SKETCHBOOK

concept sketch by Colleen AF Venabl

First Second

Text copyright © 2012 by JT Petty
Illustrations copyright © 2012 by Hilary Florido

Published by First Second
First Second is an imprint of Roaring Brook Press,
a division of Holtzbrinck Publishing Holdings Limited Partnership
175 Fifth Avenue, New York, New York 10010
All rights reserved

Distributed in the United Kingdom by Macmillan Children's Books, a division of Pan Macmillan.

Cataloging-in-Publication Data is on file at the Library of Congress

First Second books are available for special promotions and premiums.
For details, contact: Director of Special Markets, Holtzbrinck Publishers.

FIRST
EDITION

First edition 2012

Book design by Colleen AF Venable
Colored by Hilary Sycamore and Sky Blue Ink,
with Alex Campbell and Danica Novgorodoff

Printed in China

10 9 8 7 6 5 4 3 2 1